Dusk and Summer

Joseph A. Pinto

Dusk and Summer

Published by Distilled Press
Printed in the United States of America

Cover Design by Debbie Boettcher
Photo of the Tolten diary by Lisa Bachhuber

www.josephpinto.com

Third Edition

ISBN: 978-0-9991127-4-8 Print

For you, Pops

Dusk and Summer

Foreword

This is fact.

Pancreatic cancer will be diagnosed in nearly 38,000 Americans this year alone and over 34,000 will die from it. It is the fourth leading cause of cancer related deaths in the US but amazingly, it receives less than two percent of the National Cancer Institute's research budget. A staggeringly low five percent of patients survive five years after being diagnosed with pancreatic cancer, yet so little is done to seek a cure. Roughly twenty-five percent of the patients manage to live for just one year—barely fifteen percent of the occurrences are caught and diagnosed early enough for the patient to be eligible for surgery.

This is also fact.

Pancreatic cancer is a merciless, savage disease. I know. I witnessed it firsthand.

It took my father from me.

He didn't tell me how to live;
he lived, and let me watch him do it."

Clarence Budington Kelland

※ The Tolten - Wreck dive - Nov. 1 (Sat.)

Meet by 5AM - boat loaded by 7AM bring
2 tanks I have been waiting for a dive like
this. Alphonse says wreck is in good condition.
Stern 45 Degrees to Starboard. Bow intact.
It had been strengthened for icy waters.
Lies on her Starboard side.

Did some Research - the Tolten started as
the Danish ship 'Lotta' but the Chilean gov't
took it over After Denmark fell to Germany,
She was torpedoed by a U-Boat about 32 miles
off Barnaget, Fri., March 13, 1942. Later
wire dragged to Rest 16 miles SE off
Manasquan Inlet.
Crazy to think German U-Boats prowled
so close to our shores ...

Sea Cargo Drive
(off 1st Ave.)
Visibility usually good to excellent!
Large breach-
easy access
TOLTEN
27 out of 28 crewmembers died.

The Good Fight

I lost my father between dusk and summer.

Perhaps he left me long before I care to admit, long before he refused his last meals, long before his spent eyes flickered like candles behind cracked panes of some forlorn, abandoned house. Before his neglected muscles jellied into the folds of his stark white hospital sheet, and the rise of his chest grew shallow and weak. Maybe it was plain selfishness on my behalf; sitting at his bedside all those times, soothing his ears with encouragement as I squeezed his hand, desperate to impart the very courage and determination he had infused into me over my years. Even as he relied on me to raise a flimsy plastic cup of ice water to his parched lips. Had I become too scared to realize or just too blinded to ask: *whose fight did this now become*?

"...find me...from Tolten..."

I could have dismissed the words from his cracked lips as merely disoriented chatter, but his mouth pursed them too purposely, his tone too firm. Still, my father's words jolted me from my bedside vigil. I bent over his thinning form, promptly taking his hand into mine.

"...go...now," he croaked, his strength fading.

I held my breath, dared not speak. Gently, I massaged his fingers, marveling how thick and calloused they remained; my own always a child's within their clasp. Typical blue-collar hands, fearless of toil and grime. My father squeezed back, eyes widening. His candlelight flared, sparked brilliantly a moment before blinking away. I knew then I had been wrong. Someone remained home inside that deteriorating body after all. My father hung on, refusing to surrender. But what little had spilled from his lips now hung heavy between us. The message became clear. My father would not leave me.

Not until I finished his business.

My throat constricted as a terrible heat swelled within my chest. I gritted my teeth, blinked furiously and choked back the tears best as I could. Eventually, I eased him into continuing. A corner of his mouth curled. It gained momentum, spreading across his lips, his smile warming me. From within his cocoon of pillows, my father nodded his approval.

I leaned close, carefully straightening the air tube dangling from his nose. Caressed his cheek, returning his smile as his short, white stubble tickled my palm. Swallowed another blistering lump deeper into my throat. "Tell me what you want me to do, Pops," I whispered.

*****

I listened very intently to the scarce words my father pushed from his lips. *Go. 141 Sea Cargo Drive. Manasquan. You'll know. Go now.* He did not tell me what I would find or even what I needed to do. He held the obvious trust that I would just as soon figure it out, and I was not about to question or let him down. I kissed his forehead, told him I would leave, that I would see him later. From the moment my father became sick, goodbyes no longer existed. Only *see you laters.* As I forced myself from his sallow room, he cleared his throat. *Must find me...she... come back from Tolten.* I froze, deluged with fear and for the very first time a sense of hopelessness as I questioned, but for a moment, the sanity of his words, the tenuous grip he maintained upon his own reality. No; I would have none of that. I squared my jaw, turned and measured my father. I did not see a sick and dying man. The matted wisps of white hair that returned after his last bout of chemotherapy were gone, transformed into thick, luxurious curls of chestnut locks brushed back in heaps. The sagging skin of his arms now tight, bulging with muscle, the tattoos acquired while stationed in the Air Force as crisp and fresh as the day they were etched. Shoulders squared, again capable of carrying the world as he had done so many times before. Chest, wide and broad—within, the power of a Titan, the pride of a lion. Skin so vibrant and pure. His sickness did not diminish his stature. My father grew before my eyes, every day

- 3 -

becoming more the man I had known. I nodded, determined to accomplish what he needed of me.

I nearly collided with the nurse as I left his room. "Oh, I'm so sorry!" she exclaimed.

"No, it was me. I should've watched where I was going."

Her thoughtful eyes washed over me. "How are you holding up?"

My father's nurse was one of the better ones and tended to him with sincere compassion. Painfully, I had encountered too many who believed my father was just another room number. I regarded her nameplate, my gaze lingering. Dawn. Normally I would have little difficulty remembering. I had seen enough of her— every day for the past week, too many, many times over the past months. All that while, I found it easier to address her with simple hellos, with downcast, fleeting glances. I disassociated myself from the moment she entered his room. For my own self-preservation, I could not bear to voice her name. I had no choice. To do so would have thrown me under the remorseless incandescent glare of reality and I liked it where I was, alone, lost within ignorant shadows. There I could disguise life; the curtained obscurity made things not so real. It took all I could do from dropping my head upon her shoulder and weep. The shrug I managed in response drained all that remained of me.

Hesitantly, Dawn lifted her hand, carefully rested it along my arm. Gave me a soft but reassuring stroke, then slowly pulled away. "The morphine drip you requested is working as well as it could right now. Your dad has been unbelievable, you know. Joking nonstop, up until…"

My features shifted. She read it well. No luxury of morphine existed to mask my own pain. Dawn stole a look down the hall. No one approached. "Has the doctor seen you recently?"

"No more than he needs to, I guess."

She offered a sad smile. "You should know your father's kidneys are failing. His… the truth is his entire body will eventually shut down. That's why his arms… they flop when he tries to raise them. His speech—"

"Incoherent," I interrupted. *Tolten. Tolten. Come back from Tolten.* "That is, when he can speak."

An uncomfortable moment passed. An eternity gutted my soul. "We've done all we can. But this is…you need to know this is the last stage. We're keeping him as comfortable as we can right now."

She must have believed I was strong enough to handle it. Wise enough to see the writing upon the wall. She knew little of my father's resolve however, nor of the spirit I lent him all these months, and I was not about to quit.

Eventually, even a fool must realize when one's own hand cannot bend fate. No matter how hard you try. "I appreciate all you've done. I really do." I gritted my teeth. "That's a tough sonofabitch in there."

She nodded. "And a good son out here."

Tolten. Come back from Tolten. My father's words haunted me. It was time for me to go. "Can I ask a favor of you?" I said.

"Yes, anything."

"You have my cell phone number in your contact list. Call me first should... should you need to. But not my mother. Please, spare my mother."

"Of course," she answered slowly.

Shuffling away, I whispered, "Thank you, Dawn." It was at that moment I was dragged from the shadows. Things suddenly became all too real.

Open Road

Numb to the core, I curiously watched the foreign appendages attached to the steering wheel. To the left, to the right they twisted, occasionally jabbing at the directional to signal a lane change. My mind had dulled since leaving the hospital for home to collect some things before hitting the road, rendering me a puppet, aware of my actions but oblivious to whom pulled at my strings.

Lifting a shaking hand to my feverish brow, I wiped at sweat trickling down my temples, pooling under my eyes. Before me, the parkway yawned endlessly toward a shimmering horizon. Each weary glance into the rearview mirror revealed splintered, black asphalt crumbling off into the bowels of the earth. The sky above seemed to buckle, and I tensed, expecting at any moment for it to fracture like a thin pane of glass. I strained to hold myself together. Oblivious of the road, I threw my face into my hand as the first sob pinched the soft flesh of my throat. I suddenly lost the strength, the will, to keep at my journey, to remain upon the intended path. What did it matter anyway? My father lay dying and now his limbs, his very hands that served him so loyally his entire life cruelly betrayed him. I could not bear his agonizing erosion any longer and yet, day after day, I stood witness to it all. Helpless. Useless. It was not supposed to be this way. My father was only sixty years old. Too many Sundays remained watching and discussing football, Friday nights out sharing drinks like college buddies. Too many opportunities to call and ask him over my house to help fix stuff. Any kind of stuff. It did not matter, as long as he was there. And grandchildren? Did he not deserve to someday hold my child? Someone… please tell me this was a heartless prank. My father…only sixty years old.

Horns blared. My body became my own once again. My head snapped up, and I swerved recklessly back into my lane, clammy hands wringing the wheel. Took a deep breath.

Too much time remained.

I expelled the wind from my lungs, and for a sickening moment I thought I had struck an animal of some kind as it crossed the parkway, its tortured wail rising higher and higher within my truck until my ears popped and my eyes bulged. But it was me. Only me.

Time slipped away.

"Come on, Dad! Come on, Dad!" My fist beat upon the steering wheel. Eventually my howls subsided. My fever disappeared. The drone of the truck's tires pacified me. I cracked the window for some air. "I'm not giving up," I whispered to the open road. "Don't you."

Wrenches

"What are you doing?" my father asked.

I barely heard him slip through the garage door. "Sneaking up on me?" I kept my voice even, hoping he had not noticed my shoulders as they jerked in surprise.

"Of course," my father answered. "I scared you, didn't I?"

Nothing escaped my father. I could hear the huge grin in his voice even without turning around. I lied anyway. "No," I said half-heartedly.

His slippers scratched the floor as he approached. "Grown men don't show fear," he said. "They never panic. Remember what I always say…"

"I know, I know." I turned and noticed the wisps of white hair peppering the top of my father's head. It seemed so odd, out of place, to see it there, to glimpse it at all. The first signs that age had managed to track him down. Tough ox that he was, he would manage to outsmart it. He would find a way. He always did. "When you see me panic, then you panic." I pulled at the whiskers of my goatee, thumbing unconsciously at my own white streaks that had surfaced some time before. I've never seen you panic, I wanted to tell him, but I held my tongue for fear of sounding too thoughtful, a bit too tender, and my father and I never shared moments like that. Not that love did not exist between us; it remained hidden, just under the surface, just out of sight. We both knew it was there. As I matured, it seemed more special that way, rare, like a treasure chest buried in the sand. There was no need for shovels. I knew just where to find it. "Maybe if you hadn't scared the crap out of me with all those vampire movies when I was little."

My father twisted his fists at the corners of his eyes. "Boo-hoo," he sarcastically lamented. As sudden as a lightning strike, his back stiffened. "Now, are you going to tell me what you're doing?"

"I was looking for a nine-sixteenths wrench."

My father always saw through my lies. You would think as I got older that I would know better. He cleared his throat. "My toolbox is over there."

I stood at least six feet from his toolbox. "Well, I *started* looking for a wrench to borrow," and offered a sheepish smile. At least that much was true; my father owned enough tools to stock several service bays in a mechanic's shop. I barely got by with a flathead and Phillips screwdriver in my own home. "I never noticed that big file back there."

I swept my hand over a long, wooden shelf my father had built and anchored into the concrete wall of the garage. Tons of junk hunkered down atop it, but it was my father's junk, and that meant he knew where it all belonged. He could locate any item, down to a simple woodscrew, with just a few clicks of the filing system inside his mind. It also meant my fingers had traversed where they did not belong. "It's none of your business." My father's voice went flat. "That's why it's kept hidden."

"In the garage?" I asked incredulously. I may have been a grown man, but still I spoke cautiously in my father's presence. Rarely did I test our boundaries, ever mindful of the deep respect he commanded. I decided to push it a little. "Seems a little strange to hide something in the garage, don't you think?"

He bunched his brows together. "I'm the only one who can get to it. You think your mother or sister is going to come out here looking for anything, especially after telling them I see a mouse run through here from time to time?"

My father's logic, as always, remained foolproof. "You're right," I conceded with a shrug.

"Of course I'm right," he chuckled. Without warning, his face turned to stone, like a chalkboard wiped clean. "You weren't meant to see it. Not now. Maybe not ever."

"Huh? But I haven't seen anything," I protested. "I was just looking through your fishing gear, and then I saw…" I nodded my head toward the crumpled accordion file holder that captured my interest, swollen grotesquely from its enormous content contained within. Guilt overcame me; I allowed my words to dangle, hoping he would take the bait and realized it was an underhanded thing to do.

Somewhere, forgotten between pages of lore, there must exist a tale where the fish outsmarted the fisherman. My father bit into the bait and nearly tore the rod from my hand. He reached past me, thick fingers pushing through his collection of crumpled cardboard boxes, plastic containers and tattered plastic bags. Past the tools, the beaten boxes of nails, the old scuba fins and mask. He managed to clamp down upon the accordion file, nearly crushing its worn-out skin in his steely grasp, yet still lifted it gingerly and deftly from its dusty and cramped quarters. "Here. Take this." The tension squeezing his voice confirmed my assumption there was more than a meandering collection of notes contained within the file. I unfolded my arms and awaited the bundle, but instead my father cradled it like a baby against his chest. With great deliberation, he unwound the cord binding the file together and peeled the top back, thumbing through its contents with several grunts and nods. Eventually, he found whatever he was looking for.

My father tugged a red booklet, held tight by a rubber band, from the file and handed it to me. I reached for it, but he refused to loosen his grip. "You take this home and hide it. Like I have. In your basement, your attic, your own garage. I don't care, as long as it stays hidden. You tell no one that you have this. I mean no one."

Bewildered, I shook my head. I had gone into my father's garage looking for a wrench, and natural, innocent curiosity got the better of me. Maybe I should have minded my own business. This exchange was anything but expected. Far from it. The air between us grew somber. "Now listen to me carefully," he continued, "one day you may have to do something for me, and you'll find what you need inside here. Just read my notes. You should figure it out. Never, never open this until you need to. *Never*. Do you understand?"

"I… I have no idea… what are you…" I stammered, tongue lodged between my teeth. My father silenced my rant as he sliced the air with his hand.

"*You* found this. Now, can I trust you?"

"Yes," I whispered.

He leaned close, so close his breath pulsed against my face. "Then you hide this, never open its cover, never read what's inside, forget this moment completely, until the day comes that I need you, and then you'll know." My father relinquished the booklet from his grasp and backed away. My arms trembled as if it weighed a hundred pounds; it tingled oddly against my skin. A trickle of sweat hurried down my back. My father glanced at his empty palm, clenched and unclenched his fingers. Something crossed his face, a leaden shadow washed with foreboding. But it vanished hastily and left me grappling with what I thought I had just seen. "So, do you understand?"

"Yes."

"Good." My father turned on his heel as if nothing had happened, slippers scratching back across the garage floor like the imaginary mice he had warned my mother about. "Don't forget about your wrench," he called over his shoulder and went back into the house.

I forgot all about my wrench that day; I did not forget to hide his book.

Knapsacks and Signs

The shrieking draft of wind through the open window slapped me from my daydream.

My grip relaxed upon the wheel. I shifted my gaze toward the passenger seat, momentarily fixing my attention upon the knapsack laying there. I had not emptied it in months. Inside, a writing pad, fresh, empty. A pen. Wrapped snuggly in a swathe of paper towels, a bottle of Scotch.

Along with the red booklet that had once belonged to my father.

One day, you may have to do something for me, and you'll find what you need inside here.

I dragged a hand across my face, exhaled tension into my palm. That afternoon in my father's garage occurred many years before, but it reappeared in my mind as clear as the road yielding ahead of me. All these years... his booklet, hidden in my own house, taped with care to the bottom of my office desk where I sat for several hours nearly every day, until it eventually receded from my memory like the ocean's tide.

... forget this moment completely, until the day comes that I need you, and then you'll know.

The day arrived, and my father's words were as true as the sky was blue. I *did* know.

I warily eased the booklet from the knapsack as I drove, tenderly stroked its cover with great reverence.

Thumbed the fuzzy divots left across the Manila where I had peeled the tape away. Its charade of innocence attempted to work my mind over, but I knew better than to give in to its spell. I still could not comprehend the significance contained within—had my father not been so stern with his instructions, so chillingly grave, I would have dismissed it as a prank, some wild goose chase designed to leave me spinning in circles, chasing my tail. I could not dismiss that it occurred so many years before when he was healthy, whole. Of rational mind.

Now, can I trust you?

"Yes," I answered the empty space around me. I had to see it through. For him. In an hour, no more, no less, I would be reaching my destination. I would pull the rubber band from its delicate and faded cover and finally learn whatever my father had intended for me.

I drove on.

*****

Instantly, I spotted the modest sign atop its wooden post from the road. 141 Sea Cargo Drive.

I will not lie. As I turned into the long, white pebbled driveway, relief and a measure of shame drizzled across my cheeks like rain from a passing cloud. The address *did* exist. My voyage, gaining in credence, settled a bit heavier upon my shoulders. I traveled down the winding driveway, pebbles skipping and crunching beneath the tires, until I happened across a tall iron gate. It seemed too high for any person to scale and only inches existed between its bars to attempt to squeeze through, but one side of the fence lingered open as if expecting my spontaneous arrival. I passed through with little difficulty, noticing for the first time its white, cracked paint, the spider web network of rust crisscrossing its bars and remarked on its poor maintenance under my breath.

The house, as it came into view, discouraged me. Similar to the gate; neglected and worn. Its roof dozed exhausted atop its walls. Drab stucco, rupturing in patches of wide fissures, drowned midst its own sallow wash. No matter the brightness of day, this house would be lost in a swathe of dismal clouds. Hazy grime swirled windows noted my arrival with little interest, unblinking, unmotivated. Pine trees loomed large, framing it on either side, serving as loyal guardians for its unsightly companion. Or perhaps they simply stood to contain the ugliness within from escaping into the neighborhood.

I winced, brought my truck to a stop. Folded the directions I printed off the internet for this eyesore of a structure and crumpled it into the glove box. "Where did you bring me to, Pops?" I muttered, then sat, studying the house for any sign of movement. It was as still as it was shoddy. I saw no other vehicles in the drive, noticed no indication of a garage. Before I realized what I was doing, I bounced from the truck, darted up the gravel path to the front door. There were no stairs. The doorbell, or what remained of it, hung like a bulbous spider from a web, dangling on a sliver of wiring from the side of the door. Obviously, this house had not seen company in some time. A quick glance of the door – no knocker. My knuckles instead rapped upon it. Waited.

The summer sun, still infantile in the month of June, nonetheless crawled past the pine branches and raked its fingers across my neck. I swatted at the sweat beading behind my ear. Waited. Waited. I approached the door again, knocked several more times, each with greater urgency and impatience, stinging the skin across my knuckles. Two minutes. Three. I glanced at my watch. *Rap. Rap. Rap-rap.* Nothing. No one home.

I backed from the door. Collected my thoughts. The sun dazzled from its perch; my skin crawled uncomfortably under the collar of my shirt. I pulled at it, yanked at it, anything to pry the fabric from the small pool of sweat steadily collecting in the crease of my collarbone. My armpits grew damp. "Calm," I hissed, "stay calm. And *think*." Only after stemming my anxiousness did I succeed in my reasoning. I nearly slapped myself across the head. In my haste, I had failed to read my father's booklet.

Just A Book

North Atlantic Diver's Association.
North Atlantic Diver's Association.
North Atlantic Diver's…

I must have read the title of the booklet over a dozen times. A dozen times and the logic appeared no clearer. This had to be a mistake. My father had given me the wrong booklet, or maybe I had fallen for one of his practical—*Just open it.*

I checked the rearview mirror. The driveway remained quiet; the probability anyone would be arriving anytime soon seemed remote, at best. I would be on my own to make sense of it all.

… then you'll know. You'll know.

I cradled the booklet as if it was a carton of eggs. Carefully, carefully… I removed the rubber band… rested it upon my lap… the pages, so thin, flimsy… turned the cover delicately, delicately… would it withstand my touch..?

At long last, my father's booklet lay exposed. It did not radiate beneath me like the lost ark; angels did not sound trumpets from their heavenly lofts. It was just a book—pages mourning their former luster, pages humbled by coffee spots and stains. Just a book.

But my *father's* book!

I peeled back the first few pages, a log of dates from August through October, briefly detailing various events. I scanned an entry:

Aug. 23, Sat – Shark River Inlet – Night Dive

High tide is at 9:23 P.M. Meet at Todd's at 7P.M. Bring 1 tank.

On and on similar entries went—night dives, wreck dives. Dives for scallops. I could barely contain the smile creasing my lips. My father lived for this stuff when I was a young boy and he tireless. Just how old had I been? Five? Six? I cannot recall my father leaving for any of his weekend excursions, but I do remember him coming home. Always, he returned with something for me. Golden, plump starfish stored in mugs; shells, some shattered, some whole. Lobsters scurrying within his enormous fishing cooler to be boiled and eaten later on. I would sit, legs crossed, wide-eyed as he placed fragments of wood, sometimes twisted pieces of ruined metal into my cupped hands and speak of how he picked them from the wreck he had just dove. Something twinged deep inside me as though a nerve had been plucked, and tingles coursed from my neck down to my fingertips. A spark of recollection.

My father told me a story when I was a child. In the recess of night, he parted my bedroom door, tenderly lifting me from bed. I breathed deep the salt air still clinging to his skin and hair and nestled my head into the safe nook of his shoulder, lost between slumber and a dream. He shared with me a story; a story he only shared once...

I teetered on the edge of something. I forced my eyes shut, squeezing all I could from that image, demanding more. It was a connection to whatever my father's booklet held. I was certain of it and desperately needed more. Needed it *now*.

Take a deep breath. Relax. You will not get it this way. Focus.

I thumbed through more pages; directions to a boatyard off Route 36, a table of tides for Sandy Hook, dated 1975. Two illustrated pages of filleting fish, sharpening knives. By chance, at least a dozen sheets separated themselves from the remainder of the booklet. I pulled them free.

The pages were stapled neatly, creating a spine of sorts along its edge. A booklet within a booklet. The cover page read *Reefs and Wrecks* and below it a crude drawing of a sunken vessel beneath pencil scratched waves. Once more, I slowly closed my eyes and exhaled. This time my memory flowed unhindered.

Wave People

My father once told me a story when I was a child. In the recess of night, he parted my bedroom door, tenderly lifting me from bed. I breathed deep the salt air still clinging to his skin and hair and nestled my head into the safe nook of his shoulder, lost between slumber and a dream.

My feet dangled in air. I may as well have been drifting upon a cloud. The room was dark, far darker than what I was used to. My father's body blocked out my night-light but I was not scared. I felt his arms ripple as he hugged me, the swell of his chest I wished someday would be mine. I locked my thin limbs around his neck, resting within the embrace of a giant. A content moan slipped from my mouth as the tangy scent of my father's essence carried me to a place I had never been.

His grip tightened. I lifted my head, but gently he eased me back against his shoulder. "Ssh," my father cooed. "Go back to sleep."

I did not, but I closed my eyes until my body went slack and the stillness of the room filled my ears. My father rocked me, back and forth, to and fro, like the waves of the deep sea he spoke of in revered tones. He must have thought I did fall asleep for his hold loosened; I merely rode the crest of dreams.

"I didn't think I was coming back today," he whispered. He sounded worn and heartsick, but he pressed on. "Double checked, triple checked my gear on the boat. Nothing appeared wrong. I would've seen it. But I had a strong feeling not to dive. Real strong. Went against my gut and ignored it.

"About forty feet down, the feeling came back, bad, deep, deep in the pit of my stomach. I kept descending anyway. The water turned real murky, like I'd swam through a freaky oil slick. Never seen anything like it. Then it hit me… vertigo, I don't know what it was… I couldn't tell up from down. Lost sight of my diving buddy. I thought the wreck lay below me, but suddenly I felt as if I'd been swept by a current and carried miles away. Couldn't read my instruments. Couldn't get any bearings. Then, without warning, without rhyme or reason, my oxygen just cut out.

"It happened so quick, I didn't have time to react, to think. Said goodbye to you and your mother. Thought I was a dead man. I could do nothing, and didn't fight it."

My father paused. He swallowed with effort, his heart thumping against my ribs. By this time my eyes parted; I knew he could not see me in the darkness, would not know I still clung to a thread of awareness. I waited for him to say more although I could not quite comprehend what he was telling me. Weird shadows bounced across my walls; like waves, they undulated, swelled against the pale ceiling until gradually receding back toward the floor. I thought I glimpsed something—wave people, their shapes undistinguishable but somehow bobbing there, beckoning me with gestures of their hands. They meant me no harm; had I been fully awake, I would have liked to play with them. They slipped away, under the molding, into the floor. I closed my eyes and slipped with them into another half dream. My father cleared his throat.

"Before I closed my eyes for what I thought would be the last time, something... big, it swam past me. I couldn't see it at first, but I sensed it. I could feel the water part in its wake. And then...it swam past me again, and this time I could make out its shape. It was dark... darker than the crazy slick-thing that swallowed me up, darker than any moonless night. The last thing I remembered was its tail...its enormous tail... When I regained consciousness, I was floating on the surface of the water."

Lifting my head from my warm perch I asked, "Was it a shark?"

His rocking ceased. Eventually, he lowered me back into bed. Tucked the covers snugly around my shoulders. "Something like that," he answered after some length and much deliberation. "Something like that. But I'm giving it up. I'm done diving. I can thank the Tolten for that."

He kissed me upon the forehead, faded from my room. I smiled, thinking he had gone off to play with the wave people and fell back to sleep.

Wrecks and Letters

I brought my hand over my mouth.

Must find me… from Tolten…

Swiped at the pages; a table detailing east coast artificial reefs. No, that was not what I was looking for.

Flipped furiously at the pages upon my lap.

Another illustration of a broken vessel beneath the waves. The U.S.S. San Diego. I skipped over the paragraph accompanying it.

Keep searching.

The Oregon. The Black Warrior. The steamer Pliny.

My mouth grew dry. It had to be here. *Keep looking.*

The Iberia. The Delaware.

I fell upon the last page. My heart skipped several paces. I pushed my finger to the top of the page, inhaled and steadied myself. I knew what I would find; I was right.

The Tolten

On March 13, 1942, the front page of the New York Times carried this headline: "Chilean Freighter Sunk Off Our Coast – 27 Lost, One Saved"

The Tolten was traveling in ballast to New York when she was struck by a pair of German torpedoes fired from the U-404. Within six minutes, she sunk to the bottom.

Today she rests 16 miles southeast of the Manasquan Inlet in 90 feet of water. Her stern superstructure remains intact and comes up very high off the bottom.

I dragged myself from the remainder of the article. This was the wreck my father dove, some thirty-two years before. The dive that nearly cost him his life. The day he rid himself of his fins and mask forever.

The sea, however, he could never lose. That would be within him always.

My shoulders sagged. The revelation drained the energy from my limbs. All the years that had gone by…the strange images I would have of my father from time to time, those fragmented dreams which slyly escaped me once I roused from bed, the ones where I found him trapped in a well of inky darkness, and that big, black shadow circling him, always circling…

My God, it went back to that night he lifted me from bed, that night the sea danced across my walls. But why, why did he tell me his story only to never speak of it again?

Because I was only a child. Because he thought my consciousness would bury it like a coin dug into the sand.

I stared absently through the truck window for some time. Because he knew that eventually, I would come back and remember exactly where that coin rested. Because I would know when the time was right.

That could not be it though. There had to be more.

I flipped the Tolten's entry over. Once again, my father did not disappoint me.

*****

Dear Son,

If you're reading this, then it's safe to assume that I've led you this far. I don't think you would've come across this on your own; if you have, then it's too late. I'm already gone.

You're ten years old as I write, but I won't know how old you'll be when you actually get to read this. I won't know your place in life, either. I'm doing this because I was told I might need help one day in getting home.

Maybe this is nothing but my imagination, something I concocted after a good night drinking my Johnnie Walker. Maybe not. I'm still not sure what I saw that day I nearly kissed it all goodbye. All I know is that it appears all too clearly in my dreams.

Now listen to me, my son. My intuition tells me that by the time you do read this, you'll be a man. I know you'll seek the path not paved, the path that's rough and difficult, but that's the right path. You'll be honorable and true. You'll stumble in your trials but you'll never back down, never be overcome by fear in your tribulations. You're your father's son, and you'll be a tough sonofabitch like me. I wouldn't want it any other way. Most importantly, you'll achieve all I couldn't, more than I could've dreamt for you. Sure as I'm writing this, I already know—you'll carry the torch for me. Our flame will always burn bright. You'll never drop the ball.

Here it is then—crazy and insane as it sounds—you'll go and find 141 Sea Cargo Drive in Manasquan, if I haven't already told you. The house belongs to Alphonse Ford, president of the North Atlantic Diver's Association. You'll go there. And wait. I can't say for how long. To be honest, I'm not sure at all. But what you're looking for—it will find you. You'll figure it out from there. I have faith in you. Remember, I need you to do this for me.

It's not the ending I would've thought, but no one can live forever now, can they? I take comfort in knowing my son will lead me down my path.

I love you,

Pops

She

Knapsack in hand, my father's booklet tucked safely inside, I pulled myself from the truck, legs weak and uncertain. The sensation had become all too familiar. For the fifteen months since I had learned of my father's cancer, I lived my life in perpetual haze. My attention and focus on reality flickered like a dwindling light down a long hall, the edges of perception ambiguous and murky. Mouth ran dry incessantly; across my tongue, I could derive neither moisture nor taste. My ruminations mixed and churned together like the drinks I poured to quell my distress.

His cancer walloped me across the skull. The blow numbed me at once; emotion, all feeling flash-frozen inside me like fossils entrapped within Siberian walls. I am loathe to admit, it became surreally blissful, this lack of sensitivity, this hollowness which nothing could permeate or fill. For his own sake, I clung to the hope my father experienced the same and not the hell he currently endured.

My stomach lurched. I dropped to my knees, sucking the blazing summer air into my mouth until it seared the back of my throat like a blast furnace. The first dry heave seized my gut, skulked up my spine. I tossed my knapsack to the side. Again and again, my intestines pitched violently against my ribs. Convulsions ripped through my throat. A hot strand of saliva quivered from my lip; disgusted by the sight of it, disgusted by my body's sudden cowardice, I swatted it away. "Why you, Dad?" I moaned and spit the foulness from my mouth.

You'll stumble in your trials, but you will never back down, never be overcome by fear in your tribulations.

I bit down into my cheek, ridding myself of the nausea in a dancing sparkle of white spots before my eyes. My world refocused again, the stifling sun and the wet heat and the awful enigmatic mask life wore. I straightened my clothes, reached for my knapsack, rose to my feet.

I approached the front window. Cautiously, I peered inside, mindful of keeping my nose and fingertips from marking the soiled pane, expecting at any moment a hand to clamp upon my shoulder, fingers sinking into my collarbone as a voice demanded to know of my business. I flinched in anticipation, dared a glance behind. I realized then that neighbors could neither see nor hear me. The house sat too far off the road; the surrounding pine trees provided a natural barrier. I thought this house to be part of the exclusive development I had passed on the way in, but it appeared more and more that few knew of its existence, save its festering condition. Out of sight, out of mind.

Past the grimy window, grey, squared ghosts hovered in the middle of the room, some deeper off, less discernible, haunting its far corners; forgotten soldiers at their posts. Like mournful pets, the furniture remained alone, loyally awaiting their master to come home.

It seemed safe to say that moment would never arrive.

No matter, my father's instructions were to wait. I threw a hand over my head in despair. This was crazy, just crazy. I should have remained in the hospital, helping my father with his meals, providing inspiration. He needed his nourishment. Strength. He would find a way to fight on. He had twice risen from his bed when the doctors had all but given up on him. He needed me… there, with him… he needed me…

Had my father truly needed me there, he would not have sent me away.

Once more, I slung my burden across my back; I would not allow my shoulders to slouch, regardless its weight. I moved back to the front door. Fingers curled around the knob, twisted. Yawning like the mouth of a disinterested beast, the door gave way under my hand, bumping gently against the wall. I stood there, teetering across its threshold, the stale breath of desertion and dust rushing to greet me; I gasped.

Perhaps I should have been apologetic for being an unwanted stranger inside an unwanted house, but necessity prodded me on. "Hello," I called from the doorway, then held my breath. Aside from the thunderous pounding of my heart, nothing stirred from within.

I vigilantly shut the door behind me and advanced through house, around the forgotten furniture, past the neglected walls. "Hello!" I shouted as loud as I could manage without sounding menacing. "Is anyone here? I'm looking for Alphonse Ford." I proceeded down a lonely hall, into the kitchen. The counters were bare; a cabinet draw left ajar. Water dripped from the faucet as the echo of the plunks burdened the house with an even greater sense of desolation.

I crossed from the kitchen into the middle of an open family room. It seemed the very stillness of the entire house converged upon this last room for the silence here was absolute. The room was no different from the rest, barren, expectant of something that would never come, but my attention was drawn to the view beyond a pair of smudged sliding doors—a span of beach served as backyard, the summer sky leaking into the distant sea. Temptation lured me outside.

The sliding doors were unlocked as well and within seconds, a rickety deck creaked under my feet. Across several stretches, the planking stabbed in ragged splinters, and I walked with care. At the edge of the deck, I turned and faced the house, hoping to gain some new, brighter perspective of it. Maybe in some other day this place had reveled in better times, but now it sadly squatted under the sun, a hapless creature resigned to its lackluster fate. The sky beamed a polished azure, but the pigment had been sucked from the home of

Alphonse Ford long ago. A grizzled stain amidst a perfect canvas. I shuddered even as the sun warmed my scalp. Needing to remove myself from its invasive apathy, I dashed down the deck's stairs.

I trudged across a vast, roaming dune. I could hear the faint wash of the surf beyond its slope. It soothed me somewhat, loosening anxiety's grip the house managed to impart. Dune grass swayed hypnotically in the gentle coastal breeze; the further along I walked, the denser and taller it grew. It wrapped itself around my feet, my legs. Diligently I stepped; I did not wish to trample over the vegetation. A peculiar feeling had come over me, so unlike that I discovered of the drab house; a sense of reverence and mystique, as though I strode the rows of an ancient cemetery the land had turned its back on. Now the dune grass hugged my waist, grazed my chest and back like playful children playing tag, soon towering magnificently and unexpectedly over my head, closing in on my every side, until only pockets of blue sky peeked through. Strangely, I knew that swirling wall of vegetation protected me.

Abruptly, the grass ended; several feet away, the dune's edge fell. The roar of the surf robust now in my ear, sun simmering along my neck and shoulders, I plunged over the terrace like ledge. A shower of sand chased behind until I stood upon flat beach. My lungs absorbed the salt sprinkled atop the breeze. A measure of clarity returned to my senses. I inhaled as deeply as my lungs would allow.

I came upon a rowboat, its bow wedged into a knob of sand. Tufts of stringy, dried seaweed surrounded it like an old, torn blanket; contorted driftwood scattered here and there. Yards away, the grey-crested sea lapped the shore, mixing and churning in a delicate dance.

"Hello, there."

Her voice wafted from the surf, encompassing me completely, sounding as sweet as cotton candy tasted. But hard as I searched, I saw no one. Only emeralds glittering atop the waves. Twisting round, I noticed a figure approach. The sun pounced atop my face; I could discern only a shapely, dark outline. I shielded my eyes. "Hello," I answered after some hesitation.

"It's rare to see someone along this stretch of beach. Very rare." Her voice resonated gently over the rippling swells. "A pretty little patch, isn't it?"

She approached fluidly, striding across the swash marks as though she had just risen out from the breakers, deftly stepping over strewn sea debris, limbs floating gracefully at her sides. "Pretty, if only you stop long enough to appreciate it. So are you stopping or passing through?"

Now less than an arm's length away, her self-assurance warmed me as though she reflected the very sun. I lowered my hand from my eyes, at once wrapped within her radiance. Her flawlessness stunned my senses. A rich, golden tone glorified her skin, so inanely smooth, melting creamily across the soft curves revealed by the strapless sundress she wore. "Excuse me?" I said.

She smiled a brilliant smile. Flashed dusky eyes—oh, the strange mottled hue that churned and swirled within, like the crest of a storm—in a slow, deliberate blink. The breeze swept inky hair across her cheek; a swarthy lock slipped across her lips. "Stopping or passing through?"

"I'm not really sure," I managed to say.

She shrugged her sylphlike shoulders. "But you must know the reason you are here. I have never seen you before."

Her exotic gaze measured me thoroughly. I shifted uncomfortably, cleared my throat. "I'm looking for someone," I said and offered my hand.

She whirled upon her heel—whether she noticed my hand extended in greeting I was not sure—and fixed her attention to the sea, sundress rippling lazily with the breeze. "I'm looking for the owner of the house behind this dune," I continued, hoping to restore normalcy to the awkward situation. "I believe his name is Alphonse Ford. Have you heard of him?"

"Yes," she answered immediately, casting me a sideways glance.

"You have? Is there any way you can—"

"He's dead."

I staggered backward as if a tidal wave were about to devastate the shoreline, the implication too hopeless to bear. My heart plummeted; I had failed my father, failed to fulfill his wishes. Years he had waited for their possible undertaking; an extraordinary measure of faith and confidence bestowed upon me, now ruined. Dishonored. It would haunt me forever.

Her admiration of the sea hardly waned as she ignored my strangled sob. "He has been dead for years," she snapped. "You should have surmised as much after sneaking about the inside of his house."

"The door was open," I said hoarsely. "I entered only in the hopes of locating Mr. Ford. I touched nothing."

"But there is nothing to touch. You likely brushed past more ghosts than you did furnishings. Little has changed since last I was inside."

"You've been inside?"

"Many years ago. The house was different then."

"What was your relationship with Mr. Ford?"

"That hardly seems appropriate to ask," she huffed. "Especially in light of you trespassing upon private property."

"But I didn't," I pleaded. "I was instructed to come here."

She flinched ever so slightly. "Go on."

"It wasn't my intention to trespass. I give you my word that I didn't vandalize anything inside the house or the property. Look, I should just go. I can't possibly explain why I came here and have it sound sensible to a complete stranger."

"Who told you to come here?" she demanded.

I could feel the grains of time escaping through my fingers as I shifted nervously leg to leg. Tightening my clasp upon my knapsack, I remembered my father's instructions. *And wait. I can't say for how long. To be honest, I'm not sure at all. But what you're looking for...it will find you. You'll figure it out from there.* "My father. He told me to come here. Told me I would figure out the reason why. Once it found me."

A lengthy spell passed. "Let's talk at the sea's edge," she blurted, leading me by the hand as if I was a child.

*****

We stood, the sand dark and compressed under our feet as the sea lapped just beyond our toes like an eager puppy desperate for our attention. I noticed for the first time that she did not wear shoes or sandals; she curled her feet into the sand, occasionally revealing translucent toenails glowing delicately like pearls. "I'm something of a caretaker for Mr. Ford's property now, so I'm quite protective of it."

Had the tang of the sea's essence affected my judgment? Her fingertips agonizingly grazed the top of my hand, nearly hovering, poised to grasp me had I wandered free. But I could not pull myself away. A shudder tickled my spine, and I hoped she would not notice the effect her silken touch created. "I had no relations with Mr. Ford… Alphonse," she continued. "I was not a member of his family. Not his wife or his mistress, for that matter. The sea was his passion. He had time for little else. The sea, however…it always took care of Alphonse in return. When he wasn't sailing it, exploring or admiring it, he spent his time alone. When eventually he fell ill, he had no choice but to bid goodbye to his love. It was a tragic thing, and the hole in his heart never mended. So I came to him. I became his confidante. He allowed very few into his life, you see. We shared many things when we spoke. Usually the sea, his beloved, more often than not."

"It sounds like he was a guarded man. Wasn't he also president of a diver's association?" I pressed. "I would think he had many associates, friends…"

"Alphonse picked his own members. A handful, at most. Only those who shared the same interest, his same desire of the sea." The breeze amused itself within her hair. She turned, measuring me with those mystical, churning eyes. "As I understand it, he chose only the best of men."

A smile wiggled across my lips. So much of my father remained that I wished to learn. There was a reassuring squeeze upon my hand; then she pulled away, leaving me grasping for her warmth. "So it was your father that sent you here?" she asked.

"Yes."

"And why is he not present?"

My gaze shifted to my sand crusted shoes. "He's in the hospital. Very sick."

Her gaze narrowed. Suddenly fluttering her hand upon a salty gust, she crooned, "Have you ever dreamt of shedding your clothes, your cares and leaping into the waves, surrendering yourself to a fate of floating endlessly upon the great crests? Such a stunning thought. The sea...yours to control. The water as temperate as you wish. The ability to harness waves as if they were wild sea horses, to whip them into unparalleled frenzy or soothed into glassy placidity. The blessed gift to swim with dolphins, comprehend their very thoughts. Dare I say, call them family. You would be free of the land, this very world. You would belong only to the sea. You would *be* the sea, fluid as its currents, your heartbeat the ebb and flow of its tides." She danced then, spinning slowly in tight circles across the sand, and I could do no more than gape, transfixed, as her body undulated like the waves of which she spoke. Her arms beckoned the sea, rippling in such fashion they appeared like eels undulating through water. Watching her, an image flashed briefly— something last seen as a child as I clung to my father's shoulder, the evening he told me he would dive no more. The wave people, calling to me with phantom gestures from their phantom hands.

I nearly dropped to my knees as she stepped free from my childhood memory. "I can help you," she whispered, her lips lingering so close I could kiss them.

Fishermen Tales and Realizations

The afternoon aged prematurely, endless sun managing to tiptoe behind me. I had barely noticed.

She drew away from me again, away from the surf and back along the beach as her sundress billowed in a grand tease, revealing long, sinewy legs. "Wait," I called out.

She kept moving, joyfully skipping across the divots in the sand, circling the rowboat and eventually leaning against it. Slender fingers reverently stroked its surface as though she had set sail in it many times, fondly recalling her voyages. "When first I met Alphonse, I told him a story about this very boat. A fisherman's tale," she began once I had caught up, "that this tiny boat faithfully marks the forthcoming of a severe storm. It can be seen pitching and bobbing in the troughs of the waves at different spots along the coast, but only in the midst of twilight. Like a...phantom. Always rocking unoccupied at the sea's mercy. Those courageous enough to swim past the breakers, through the shackles of the currents to assume control of the craft...to break its very spirit as though a wild steed...then by daybreak they would be gone from this boat, gone forever. Vanished without a trace. Taken, some say, to some other magical place." She winked. "Of course, it's only a fisherman's tale."

I rested my knapsack against the hull of the craft. "My father told me something would find me here. It's you, isn't it?"

Her fingernails, luminous in the same, curious way as her toes, tapped softly against the wood.

"Who are you?"

She flipped raven hair from her face, lifted her hand from the boat and placed it against my cheek. At once, I melted and pressed myself into her palm; head held aloft upon a cloud.

She brought her face full into mine, lips a breath away as before. "Spend time with me," she cooed and slipped down to the sand, smoothing a spot beside her.

"You haven't answered me! You haven't told me who you are. Are you the one I'm supposed to find or are you just playing me? Dear Lord, I'm losing my mind." I placed a hand across my mouth, stifled a cry.

She merely patted the sand. "Sit with me. Let me tell you stories of the sea, as I've loved them. As I *know* them."

I opened my mouth to argue, but she brought a finger to her lips. "Ssh," her voice like sashaying palms.

At once, the strength evaporated from my legs. Bracing my back against the hull of the rowboat, I slid down until our shoulders touched. She nodded her approval. The horizon yawned, slowly swallowing the sun. I squeezed my eyes shut, savoring its fading warmth across my cheeks and brow. Then her stories began. Of stormy nights and tranquil days, of trade winds and sudden cyclones, of shooting stars stirring the sea and black, cresting waves washing the moon. Of captains fearless and strong sailing headstrong into the eye of the tempest. Of the husks of ghostly wrecks abandoned along the sea's floor. She told me many tales; she held me captive by them all.

And then there were stories of mermaids.

Frolicking deep among schools of exotic fish, breaching the sea's surface in emerald mists. Singing satin songs while sunning atop bleached coral reefs, brushing their shimmering bronze and strawberry and ebony hair. Of mermaid cities buried deep between the fission of canyons, of mermaid nations migrating upon the currents. Her stories seemed too unreal, too fantastic to believe, but she lulled me with her sincerity especially as she recalled, with fondness and a certain measure of pride, a mermaid race that could shed their tail upon command and take to dry land. Each possessing a unique ability, a wondrous power. Tucking my legs into my chest, I wrapped my arms round my knees and listened like a child sitting beside a campfire. Her words poured into me, filled my chest with warmth as if I had just drunk brandy. All of time, all my beliefs were suspended, and I did not wish for her to stop. I absorbed her every word, felt as though I could touch the canvas she brushed so meticulously inside my head. Eventually she did stop, her mermaid stories came to a whispered end, breaking my trance. My eyes snapped open. Had I somehow fallen asleep? Had I imagined the worlds she conjured as her own? I stared into her perfect face, awash in the ebb of a melting sky.

"I could bask in dusk forever," she sighed. "Yes, the sun may set but soon night thrives. Comes alive." There was no denying my mysterious companion's words. I could almost sense a faint heartbeat...*there*, above the din of the tide. As if one entity ceased to be and one now survived.

We watched the day dissolve for good. Eventually, brilliant twinkles of light peeked through the raw gloaming overhead. In the distance, the dune grass kept in hushed tune with the breeze. She hummed along.

"What have you brought?" she asked abruptly. "In your bag?"

I had nearly forgotten about my knapsack. I shifted uncomfortably against the boat.

"Tell me."

"It's nothing, really."

"Tell me what is inside," she insisted.

"Just notes. My father's notes that got me here."

"There must be more. Tell me."

"I don't want to talk about it!" I snapped. She threw me a sideways glance, then busied herself scanning the glittering jewels of moonlight wavering atop the inkiness of the sea.

We sat at length in the sand. Exchanged no words. All the while, a horrible, smothering pressure built within my chest. No matter my attempts to gulp the evening's fresh, cool air, my lungs would not expand. The sky caged me on all sides; chest heaved as a monstrous panic attack seized me. My limbs frantically twitched and thumped like a fish floundering on land. I bounded from my spot, an explosion of legs and sand, scampering as fear's tentacles curled round my arms, squeezing tight across my ribs, wrapping round my legs as hideous beak-like pucker mouths tore at my flesh. Driftwood caught between my lumbering feet; down I went in a frantic heap. Grainy pavement smacked my face; sand choked my nose, my mouth. With what remained of my strength, I managed to flip onto my back.

And there I lay. The rising tide thundered not far from me; mere feet and then inches, it seemed. The sea's fringe groped for my head. I held my breath and prayed for the next great wave, swelled to unparalleled prominence, to consume my body into its frothing wrath. Prayed for it to pulverize me as one into the sand, until I became nothing more than granule and grit. To sweep me away upon its black currents, where the sharks and unspeakable beasts would feast upon the remains of my bloated, decayed body. Where finally I would be no more.

I desperately wished to switch places with my father. Ending my own life seemed a fair trade-off for the man who had given up so much for me. Nothing short of my own sacrifice seemed likely to appease the gods or ensure the return of the man I knew him to be.

Not the imposter saddled in that loathsome hospital bed, not the imposter ravaged by incomprehensible disease. Not that man.

Not *my* father.

"Not my father!" I howled; a beast blinded in pain.

High above, stars winked against a ceiling sucked of all its pigment. My father's face, so ashen, so drawn, flashed between lazily emerging constellations, flashed between transient phantom-like clouds. "Do you hear me? Not my father!" I raged against the heavens, raged against whatever lay beyond. No one and nothing answered me, save for the throbbing of blood deep within my ear, the tide's crescendo drowning the hammering of my fists into the sand and the heavy, omniscient heartbeat of night. Stripped of my last securities, face smothered in my hands, I sobbed. I sobbed and did not stop. Nor would I. Not for all the riches in the world. Not until my father rose from his bed and joined me upon the beach, hand in hand, free of his oxygen tank and wheelchair. Free from the grains slipping away within the neck of the hourglass.

I felt her presence at once, like sunbeams escaping from behind clouds. She stood angelic before an emerging moon, soft halo pulsing above her head. She said nothing as she dried my tears and offered me her hand. I do not remember how such a delicate, wonderfully pristine woman pulled me to my feet, supporting my weight over mounds of shifting sand.

Somehow, she did. Somehow, she nestled me back to where we had begun, and she sat against the boat once more with my head upon her warm lap.

I possessed not the power to push away. My arms hung at my sides, fingers curled into the sand. Her face hovered over me, pitch-black hair plummeting down, dissolving into the sky. Incandescent eyes caught the newborn moon; her features shifted as if a passing cloud rearranged the subdued shadows cast by her cheekbones, her brow. I thought I glimpsed something—how can I explain—other than what she was, but the mirage vanished in an instant until she resembled the same striking beauty.

"Ssh," she cooed and drew her fingers across my face, softly tracing the shallow of my cheek. Tenderly she closed my eyelids, her touch so maddeningly delicate, like butterflies grazing my lashes. The warmth of her stroke swathed me from the growing teeth of the sea's breezy nip. Time and again, she caught my rolling tears upon soft, impassioned fingertips, affectionately wiping them away. Hushed my weakening sobs with adoring caresses of my temple. The breeze whistled higher above us now. The haunting swish of the dune grass sashay grew ever stronger. Its melody acted like a drug upon my senses, and I felt as though I floated with heavy limbs along a laggard current. I could not stir, nor did I wish to. Sluggishly, my lids closed, then parted. The dark well of sky bled into the sea; stars jittered like lighting bugs caught in a jar.

I drew my arms around her, took comfort in her waiting embrace. She pressed her body against mine, gently easing my weary head across her chest. "Ssh," and then murmured in a honey like pitch a satin lullaby. Her black, lush hair spilled across my cheek, its scent at once filling my nose. Her essence so prominent, fresh.

So familiar.

I could feel her skin quiver beneath me. Again, I became so sleepy. With each droop of my lids, I half imagined silvery mermaids with their great fins cresting the waves, diving deep, deep below the surface where the sun could not reach them, where the only light came from the phosphorescent glow of their seabed sanctuaries. There were so many, many mermaids.

I hugged her close, inhaling as deeply as I could. Pressed my nose into the crease of her neck as a child would. Breathed deep the salt air still clinging to her skin, her hair. Slowly, my eyes widened.

The same salt air I once breathed nestled in the nook of my father's shoulder, so many years before.

I gasped, shrunk from her embrace. Her song ceased. The moon illuminated her face, casting trembling slivers across her shoulders, and her eyes—those dusky, mottled eyes—gleamed with all the beauty of coral reefs, flared with the same phosphorescent glow of the undersea cities I had glimpsed.

The tide filled my ears, but I only heard my father above the din. "*I didn't think I was coming back today*," he had whispered to me.

Then it all came rushing back.

I clung to my father that night he told his tale, rocking his only son back and forth as though we bobbed upon the vast waves of the unknown open sea he longed desperately to be one with, spoke of with such grand admiration.

But it was the weird shadows swimming across my walls I remember most. The undistinguishable shapes of the wave people soaring and diving across my room. Beckoning me. Had my father noticed? I suppose I will never know. But they were there. Surely now, I have no doubt.

"It was you," I blurted, throat so dry. "You saved my father, didn't you?"

*****

She batted her lashes, her gaze casting upon me much affection.

"I come only for those who belong to the sea. That is *my* power. The gift I share."

My heart pounded within my chest.

A grave smile of empathy passed her lips; she took my hand into her own. "Many, many years ago, I happened across Alphonse Ford. I watched him from afar, as his love affair for the open sea grew endlessly since he was but a child. You see, the house you entered belonged not only to him but to his parents as well. Alphonse was raised with the sea as his playground. He spent most his days playing upon the beach, sitting and admiring its beauty.

"It was my mistake. I was careless and drifted too close to the coast. Alphonse was here, relaxing beside this very boat as was his tendency, his mind adrift, daydreaming atop the choppy sea. Somehow, he sensed me. Saw me. I could not slip back under the surface quickly enough. I swam away, but he leapt into the sea and followed. For a boy his age he was strong. Not strong enough to escape the undertow he found himself trapped, however. Almost at once, the currents swept him away, far away. I felt the vibrations of his struggles as he thrashed the surface. Against my better judgment, I rushed to his aid. Mind you, I do not interfere until one's calling is proclaimed, but he *was* only a child, and his time was not yet up. He would have perished had I not intervened. What else was I to do?

"Alphonse accepted what I was, and so I remained in his life. Occasionally, I would meet him upon the beach, speak about life and his love, the sea. Usually, I fulfilled myself simply observing him, awaiting the sad day…the day I would be summoned. By that point in time, he knew of my purpose. When finally that moment arrived, he swore me to a promise. A pact. His house, now left to him by his parents, would be placed under my guard and serve as a haven. A beacon, if you will, for those delivered into my care."

"I don't understand."

She patted my hand. "The dying come here. Then, I deliver them."

Her words hung heavy between us. "Alphonse carefully chose your father to become a member of his diver's group," she continued, "mindful that, indeed, he may become aware of my existence as well.

"Alphonse dove the Tolten with your father that day. I know all the wrecks, you see," she said proudly. "Their locations. Their histories. I've explored them all. I happened to be watching over Alphonse that day, but something pulled me...*lured* me...toward your father. I approached him, closer and closer. I remember now...the water was rather murky...I swam behind your father, so close I could have touched him. Something went wrong. I sensed distress in the water immediately. I circled your father. He was a strong, sure man, but he needed help. As it was with Alphonse, it was with your father. His time was not yet up, either. I drew close. Your father saw me. How his eyes widened. Not in fear, no. Your father had been as close to death as any man I have been around, but he showed no panic. The courage in his heart! He looked at me, *admired* me, as if I had been an angel. An angel!" She cast her sublime face to the heavens—the very heavens

I had scorned. "Often, I have wondered how it must feel to possess wings rather than fins, a tail. To soar high and dip and play between the clouds, to gaze down upon land." Stars twinkled within her musing, thunderstorm eyes. "Yes, I am guilty of such thoughts. But I must take comfort knowing that a higher power created me to wield its intentions through water rather than air."

After some hesitation, she said, "I took your father into my arms and carried him to the surface. I supported him above the pitch of the sea until Alphonse could surface. It was Alphonse eventually told him the consequence of my coming into his life."

I slowly withdrew my hand. Shivered head to toe. "And now you're here."

"I am no monster," she spoke, distress brimming within her voice. "I saved him that day. But I *am* what has been chosen to be."

"You've chosen my father!" I snapped again, rage flaring across the surface of my skin.

"No, I have not!" Her utterance carried above the crash of the waves, echoing deep into the unforgiving night. "I serve only as the vessel to deliver him home. Nothing more. I am not the cause of his affliction. I am not his cure. His suffering…it is etched so deeply into your face. I do not wish to know what he endures, and yet it's more than he deserves, I am sure. But let go of that now. Let go! Live in his glory. Live for his fight, his courage. Live for him, forever more. Your father sent you here with purpose. His intuition served him well. He knew he might not make it here on his own. He knew he might not have the opportunity to live out the remainder of his months, his days, as the others before him had. Like Alphonse. He sent you here. *You*. His son."

As I write this, I already know—you'll carry the torch for me, and our flame will never burn brighter. You'll never drop the ball.

Tears tumbled fresh across my cheeks.

Remember, I will need you to do this for me. It's not the ending I would've thought, but no one can live forever now, can they? I take comfort in knowing my son will lead me down my path...

"*He* sent you here," she insisted.

I clenched my teeth. "Please tell me what I need to do."

She smiled. "You will write for him."

Johnnie and Immortal Kisses

The stars plunged from the sky.

The breeze ceased to be, and the sea hushed at once, whimpering submissively as its surface chilled into a solid ebony sheet stretching from shore until the end of the world. It may as well have been the end of the world, too. Her words struck me with the cold finality I had been running from for the past fifteen months.

She watched my reaction carefully, her wide-eyed gaze washing over me like glittering moonlight. Surely, she noticed my body trembling like a sickly animal. I could neither hide nor prevent it. With shaking hand, I groped for my knapsack, dragging it clumsily through the sand. It felt so heavy, so foreign, in my grasp. For fifteen months, I had carried it and its contents with me. Now, I was about to cut it free like an umbilical cord. "I can't do this. I can't!"

She said nothing.

"Please," my voice cracked, "please, I beg of you, don't make me do it. Not *this*."

"Your father deserves mercy. Now grant it to him."

My father would never willingly succumb to his cancer. My hero's battle had already achieved mythical proportions. He had slain the great beast. His war should have ended. But the wounds suffered in combat were too much for even my father to overcome.

Moment by heartrending moment, I understood my role in this Greek tragedy.

Far away, as his breath drew ever shallow and his heartbeat dimmed, I realized my father awaited his earthly release by my hand.

I squared my jaw.

I love you, my champion. May my pen be far mightier than my sword.

I unzipped my knapsack, grasped my pen. Took the writing pad and positioned it across my lap. Carefully handling the clump of paper towels, I peeled free the bottle of Johnnie Walker Black from within. Where once darkness consumed me, there was now light; a soft glow of phosphorescent moon dust danced upon my lap and pad. My chest heaved. My throat constricted. Fifteen months; finally, my running had come to a halt. "I thought…I thought this should be done with a clear mind," I stammered. "I kept putting it off… it's the only reason I carried it with me. But I never dreamed…never dreamed…of *actually* doing it. To do so would have betrayed my father, betrayed his fight. It would have meant I had given up on him!" I buried my head into my hands. "I never gave up on him. Never!"

Tenderness furled around my fingers. With loving grace, she lifted my sorrowful gaze. As a mother would nuzzle her child, she brushed against my brow with her own. "Ssh. Tell me of your father as I shared with you my stories. Give him life again. Allow him to breathe. Make him *whole*."

The night returned to me. Something slipped from the cool air, surrounded and warmed me like a thick shawl. I swayed to the sea's hypnotic pulse, inhaling deeply its sharp tang as it massaged my inhibitions away. I suspended all belief, allowing myself to believe summer was real again. I was still a boy. When next my lips parted, when my pen scratched against moonlit paper, the stories became my own. I narrated with a hushed, revered tone and in slow, methodic scrawl, barely cognizant how closely my voice resembled the sea or how my words coursed with its same rhythmic cycle.

Under spectral candlelight, I shared with her a tale of a rugged, Spartan man who knew nothing but sweat-drenched labor and unheralded sacrifice all his life. A man who woke for work before the stars in the sky had yet matured; thick, hardened fingers eternally stained with soil and hardship, brandishing a dazzling array of tools as mighty Thor might wield his hammer. A man whose lofty principles overshadowed any simple wants. A man bored by the problematic, challenged by the mere prospect of impossible. A man without pretense and whose reputation preceded him.

I recounted mysterious whispers, rumors that mesmerized my senses, consumed my thoughts, captivated me when I was but a child. I did my best to impart justice to them all; those mystical accounts of the youthful man that was my father, so agile, so strong. Stories, heard with such frequency I could not easily discredit them, of his uncanny dashes across fields of competition with such fleet of foot not even Mercury could keep pace, as wings sprouted from his very ankles, skirting him elusively above the ground. The myth that the man, for lack of challenge, scaled the cliffs of Olympus itself, wrestled and pinned the flailing limbs of the gods to the lightning seared soil. It was said even Zeus himself yielded ground to my father. In turn, the gods chiseled his likeness from their mountainside, immortalizing my father's preternatural might and unrivaled valor.

The moon drew her polished cloak around my shoulders as silvery shadows cavorted across the paper, played with my pen. On through the night my stories melded, more fantastic than the last. Bolder than captains fearless and strong. More dignified than emerald mermaids swimming in their fabled ruby seas.

When at last I inscribed the final word across my pad, the pen fell from my trembling hand, and I gasped. A sensation like no other overtook me, a remarkable feeling that although my body sat upon the sand, I experienced from another. A great and oppressive weight lifted free from my chest, my shoulders. I could breathe again, truly breathe on my own, a rarified air that made my senses sing. My limbs, surging with vibrant, powerful muscle…my body…my God, my body…

"That was beautiful," she whispered. "He truly is a legend."

Fifteen months and my running was done. My father's eulogy sealed by my hand.

I took hold of my father's bottle of Johnnie Walker. Clutched his eulogy to my heart. His energy coursed through my body, filled my every fiber. Miles separated us, yet I could feel his eyes upon me, his smile grateful, warm. Somehow, I had done it. Yes, somehow...he was again whole. "Yes, he is a legend and more," I whispered, pressing his eulogy again so damn hard against my heart. "He's my *father*."

I honored him with a hearty swig.

*****

I poured the last drops from the bottle into the sand where it was sucked down in ravenous gurgles. Satisfied the interior of the bottle was sufficiently dried, I carefully rolled my father's eulogy between my fingers and sealed it within.

"I suppose you'll need this."

With pinched lips, she accepted the bottle. "This as well." I reached within the knapsack, pulling the red booklet free.

She held it to the glow of the moon, thumbed through its pages, every so often glancing up. She handed it back. "No, this is yours. All this, your father's memos. It belongs to you now." She shuffled across the sand, face full into mine. A pained expression clouded her glorious features. "Will you find your way back here someday?" Her voice trailed away.

Perhaps I will never learn the true intention of her words. But I took comfort knowing that if I were to return, in whatever capacity meant for me, she would certainly find me. "I will always remember this place," I answered softly. "Pretty, if only you stop long enough to appreciate it."

Her liquid eyes glistened; the tempest of intensity within them reluctantly mellowed. For the first time, her exquisite face appeared strained, and even she could not hide the slight quiver from her lips. Is it also said in fantasy that a mermaid can weep? I do not know that answer. Then again, should I be asked someday if mermaids were real, I would not reveal that truth either. She reached for me, brushed my cheek with yielding fingers and cupped the back of my head into her palm. Admired me with those electric, chimerical eyes not of this earth, soaking my very essence into her churning maelstrom until dear Lord I swear I would be carried in the throes of an undertow and swept far away. Then her soft, soft lips pressed against mine.

She scrambled to her feet as if her kiss was some forbidden thing. Perhaps, for the both of us, it was. Her magic lingered across my lips, and I knew then it all to be true. Her stormy eyes lingered over me a final time. In silence, she turned, clutching my father's bottle to her breast. She left me where I sat, alone, save for the peaceful melody of dune grass humming in my ear, the gritty solace of sand beneath my hand, the ever-changing disposition of waves in the recess of night and walked slowly down to the sea, peeling away her sundress, discarding it in a heap behind her. Moonlight hugged the curves of her lush, naked figure; she waded into the water as first her feet, and then her legs, disappeared amidst the breakers. Further, further as the dark sheen of sea graciously accepted her, welcomed her back home. Until she vanished from my sight.

If I could have followed, I would have. I knew it was not meant to be. Instead, I laid myself beside the rowboat, my knapsack my pillow, the stars my blanket. As my lids succumbed to exhaustion, a meandering thought occurred to me—I had never learned her name. Yet I will always remember the moment Lady Death kissed me, for it was then that I realized death played many roles and wore many faces.

Some more beautiful than you can ever imagine.

Whole

Did I influence my dreams during the night or
were they guided, perhaps, by something else?
Regardless, my father was with me. My dog as well.
Together, we walked the beach. Miles and miles of
unblemished beach. My father and I, side by side. Yes,
my father walked. Unconstrained by the shackles of the
past fifteen months. Barefoot. Relishing the sand oozing
between his toes, the cool wash of sea across his feet.
My father and I locked glances; how I admired the
ample, lavish curls of chestnut hair heaped atop his
head, the tight, bulging muscle of his biceps and
forearms rippling beneath his Air Force tattoos, now
clear and fresh as the day he had them etched. Sculpted
shoulders rivaling Atlas himself, effortlessly supporting
the weight of the world. Chest, broad and thick—
contained within the power of a Titan. The pride of a
lion. Skin aglow under the dazzling summer sun.

My father grew…he always grew before my
eyes.

Yes. My father, at last, whole.

We walked and did not share a word. There was
no need. My father absorbed our time together, the
summer…*life*, and I did not dare wish to interrupt. My
dog danced and frolicked between our feet, skipped
over the fingers of waves along the shore. My father

laughed. Oh, how he laughed. Then my dog took off running; my father turned to me, his eyes twinkling, so eager to follow. I smiled and without hesitating nodded a simple approval. My father bolted, giggling hysterically like a child, flipping somersaults under the resurgent sun, running so fast his feet barely touched the sand. Dashing and frolicking with my dog. My father scooped her into his arms, cradled her gently while splashing in the surf until they sauntered off, mere specks against a pearly beach.

The morning sun appeared like fresh yolk from a cracked egg. I must have slept with eyes wide open, for the shrill of seagulls and the mournful ring of my cell phone merely interrupted my fancies. I did not need to look. I knew who would be on the line. I knew. "Yes, Dawn," I croaked.

Sometimes, regardless your preparedness, life can drive you to your knees. "I'm so sorry," she sighed. "Your father is gone."

My phone slipped from my hand. I stumbled to the sea's edge.

My father was free now. Of that much, I was sure. I stared along the horizon's edge; I thought I glimpsed silhouettes breaching the sea's glittering surface. Silvery, magnificent figures bobbing atop the waves. Was she among them? Was my father? In my heart, yes, I hoped. How I hoped. I motioned with my hand, and they signaled back. The wave people I had glimpsed as a child. I would have liked to play with them, but it was my father's turn now.

I lay atop the sand, tide heavy in my ear, raw sun warm across my body. Dune grass murmuring a song about a champion for the ages. I will see you later, Pops.

Goodbyes never did exist.

Deep in my heart, I will mourn him always, until the moment he returns and takes me by the hand to his secret place between dusk and summer.

AFTERWORD

A tribute to my father

A fantasy is born of equal parts magic and truth; a writer's promise to his audience should be a seamless telling of the two.

I wrote Dusk and Summer because I owed my father a debt of gratitude, one a child can never truly repay a parent. A thank you for being not only the man who raised me, but a role model and hero that I now strive to be for my own daughter.

I remember a day long before he was diagnosed with pancreatic cancer when my father told me, in a dreamy kind of way, how he would like to be cremated when it was his time to go—his remains scattered across the sea. How he loved the open water. My father had been a scuba diver and only by the hand of the sea did he feel complete, her sweet whispers bringing him true peace. I like to believe that in another life perhaps, my father had been a salty fisherman or, more fantastic still, a merman of sorts. In this life, however, he'd been a man whose simple love of the ocean brought him a tranquility no other place could match.

On the day he confessed his wish to be one with the sea, we both simply nodded in silence, his want revealed, his intentions made clear. I suppose, thinking back upon it now, we both took his words with a grain of salt. My father was relatively young at the time; a bull. An unstoppable force. He wouldn't be leaving this world anytime soon. As the years went by, I never thought to question the conviction of his statement, nor did it ever dawn on me that the burden of his desire would weigh so heavily upon my shoulders.

Not even on the surreal day that he was diagnosed with pancreatic cancer did the full truth of the matter occur to me.

My father never bought into the statistics of expected survival rates, not even when cancer snorted its rancid breath into his face. For those who had the privilege of knowing him, that should come as no surprise. Some said he was the toughest sonofagun they had ever met; some said he had no equal. I can only attest to the fact that to me, he was Superman. Even with kryptonite glowing ominously before him, he never blinked or backed down from the fight.

On the day the severity of his cancer was revealed – stage four, metastasized into his liver and possibly, with some luck, only three months to live – my father turned to my mother and I and proclaimed in a firm, strong voice, "I'm taking the ball and running with it. I'm going to score a touchdown. I'm going to beat this thing." Our rally cry had been born—"*Never drop the ball.*"

That was my father. Blissfully, stubbornly, and determinedly headstrong. He jumped into all things guns blazing; he conquered all obstacles with tight lips, sleeves rolled up, soil creasing his palms and a drink waiting for him afterwards at the bar.

Against all odds, through many ups-and-downs and more suffering than any one man should be forced to endure, my father valiantly waged war against the great mysterious beast for fifteen months—conquering the expectancy the doctors initially diagnosed.

Eventually, I asked the Lord to please, *please* deliver him from his battle, but even then, my father refused to budge an inch. Even then, his strength of spirit continued to teach me—on the rare occasion, in the rare man, as the body fails, the soul grows stronger. I may be able to master many words, but I cannot possibly describe the miracle I witnessed with my own eyes. And to this day, I remain in awe of my father's inner fortitude.

I will take the following to my own grave. It was a Saturday, and several days had gone by with my father unable to articulate full sentences for his weary body was shutting down. My wife and I entered his hospital room to the anguished cries of a man in unspeakable pain. My father writhed upon his bed; his fists beat upon the sheets. As I frantically attempted to call his doctor from my cell phone in order to authorize a morphine drip, my father rose from the bed, clutched my arm and gasped, "I'm giving you the ball. You run with it now." He then lowered himself back down.

His last words to me.

I've told this tale with as much pride and love as my heart can bear; I've shared this tale until it has become mythical even to me.

My father never did make his burial intentions clear. He was laid to rest in the family plot my mother had chosen long before. But to be honest, it's never sat right with me. His wish, his want for his own remains to be joined with the sea had never been realized.

So I owed you one, Pops...and here it is. *My* way of bringing you where you've always longed to be. Where you'll always belong. I've never forgotten that day. Or your words.

I know you're with me every day, reading over my shoulder, sitting beside me, even now. It's an incredible honor to share your tale.

Know that I'll never drop the ball, Pops.

My promise always.

Thank you for Purchasing this Book

I sincerely thank you for purchasing Dusk and Summer. A portion of proceeds from this sale will be donated to the Lustgarten Foundation for Pancreatic Cancer Research.

The Lustgarten Foundation's mission is one shared by many advocates: the advancement of scientific and medical research related to the diagnosis, treatment, cure and prevention of pancreatic cancer. This means will come via increased funding and support of research, the facilitation of dialogue among members of the medical and scientific communities and a tireless campaign to heighten public awareness.

In January 2013, the Lustgarten Foundation awarded $25 million dollars in new multi-year research grants to be used developing early detection methods and better therapeutic options, and testing them with patients. At around the same time, Mayo Clinic researchers identified a new molecule to target in pancreatic cancer treatment. Each day begins a new day for hope.

It is never too late to join the fight. There are incredible amounts of ways to get involved in the fight against pancreatic cancer; organized research walks and runs, golf outings, pancake breakfasts, and even motorcycle rides are just some common fundraisers started by people like you and I. And yes, even writing a book. The Lustgarten Foundation itself hosts and supports many events such as their annual Holiday Rock and Roll Bash each December in New York City and their online feature, Gifts That Give Back.

Please don't hesitate—visit www.lustgarten.org on the internet today and further educate yourself about the mission and goals of the Lustgarten Foundation.

Joseph Pinto is the author of the poetry collections *From My Front Steps* (2021), *Scotch and Scars* (2020) and *A Distilled Spirit (2018)*, the poignant novella *Dusk and Summer (2008)* and the horror novel *Flowers for Evelene (2005)* – as well numerous dark fiction tales; his unique voice has been showcased in a multitude of anthologies and magazines as well as individually published short stories.

He is known as the barflypoet – and yes, he really writes poetry from inside bars.

Indulge in Joseph's work at www.josephpinto.com

Follow him on:

Twitter: @JosephAPinto

Instagram: @joseph_a_pinto

Facebook:

Joseph A. Pinto, barflypoet & author of dark fiction

YouTube (spoken word poetry):

Joseph Pinto, the barflypoet